THEA LEMON
AND HER SUPER SWEET
FAIRY GODMOTHER

By Mark Lemon
Illustrated By Maia Walczak

Published by Lemon Drop books

I would like to tell you a magical story about an ordinary girl named Thea Lemon. Thea lives with her Mum and Dad, in a large city called Bristol in

England. Her parents own the Lemon Drop Café
on Church Road in St. George

The cafe gets so busy, that every weekend Thea is sent to stay with her terrible Great Aunt Fellulla, who Thea secretly calls 'Craggy Bottom'. Great Aunt Fellulla has curly blue hair, wonky round spectacles, and yellow teeth. She wears brown dresses and dirty black boots. She is known by the people in her village as the kind of person who never smiles, doesn't like Christmas and is always complaining about something!

Now let me get to the story, as there is quite a story to tell. It was a cold, shivery Friday afternoon in October and Thea's school bell had

just rang to mark the end of the week. Thea and
her friends gathered in the school playground to
talk about what they were doing that weekend.

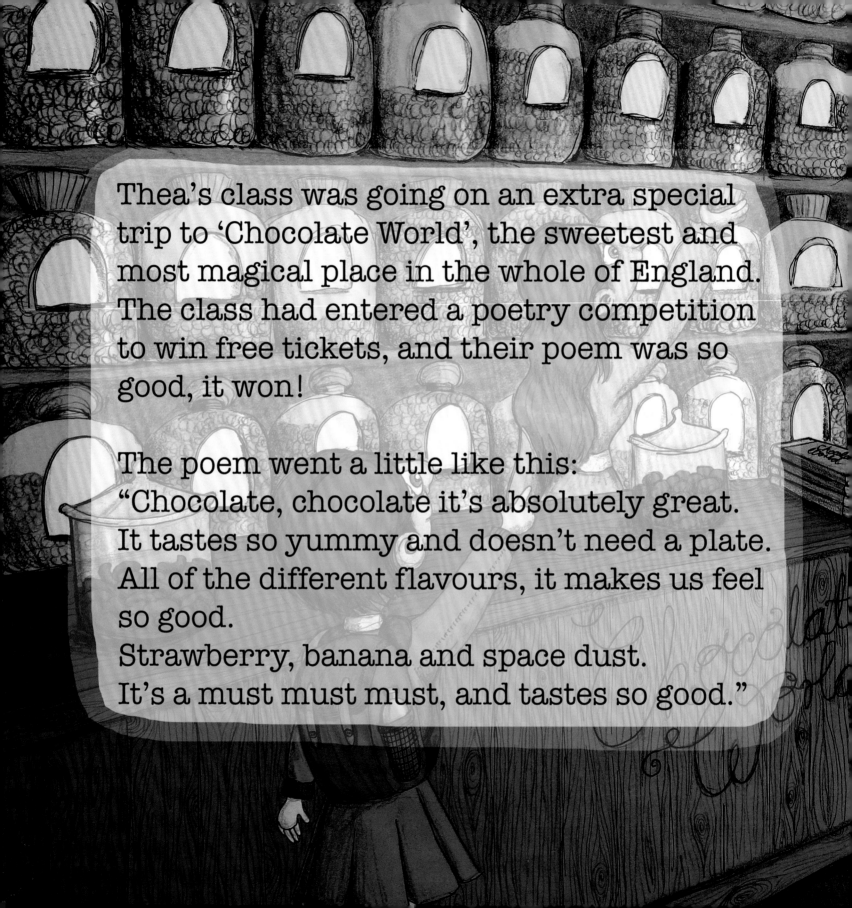

Thea's class was going on an extra special trip to 'Chocolate World', the sweetest and most magical place in the whole of England. The class had entered a poetry competition to win free tickets, and their poem was so good, it won!

The poem went a little like this:
"Chocolate, chocolate it's absolutely great.
It tastes so yummy and doesn't need a plate.
All of the different flavours, it makes us feel so good.
Strawberry, banana and space dust.
It's a must must must, and tastes so good."

Thea's friends were very excited about the trip, and all the magical things they would see, and all the chocolate they would eat.

"I can't wait for tomorrow," said Victoria Villington.

"I'm going to buy a whole year's supply of sweets," said Mary Millington.

"The coach picks us up from school at nine o'clock. Don't be late girls," said Susan Sillyman.

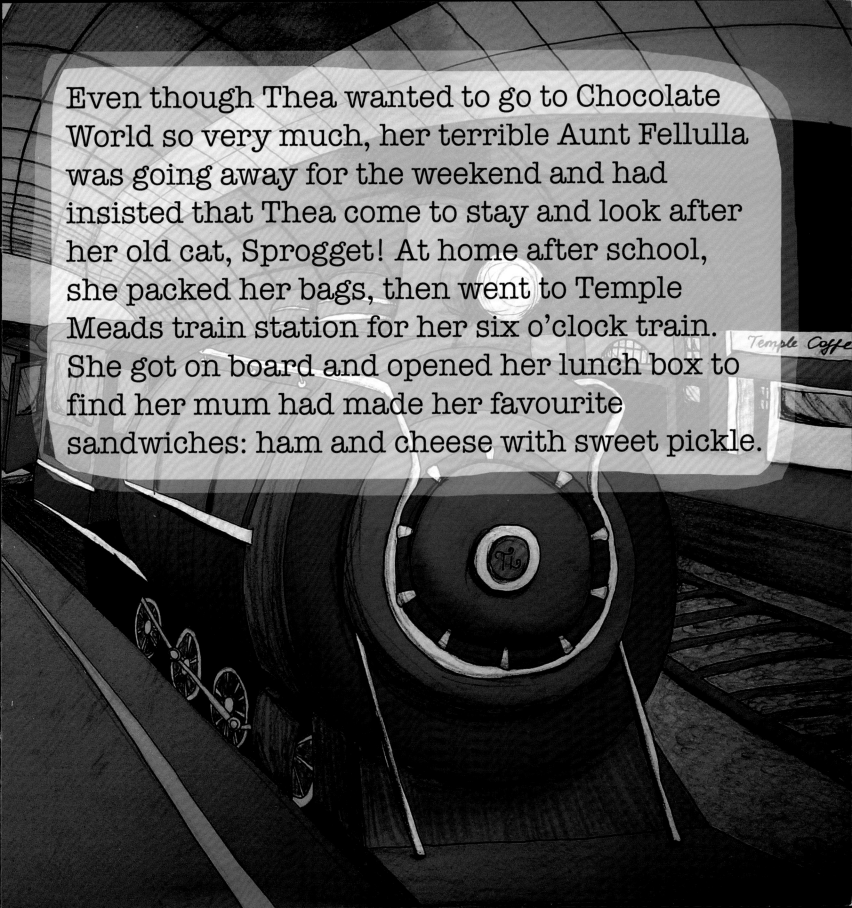

Even though Thea wanted to go to Chocolate World so very much, her terrible Aunt Fellulla was going away for the weekend and had insisted that Thea come to stay and look after her old cat, Sprogget! At home after school, she packed her bags, then went to Temple Meads train station for her six o'clock train. She got on board and opened her lunch box to find her mum had made her favourite sandwiches: ham and cheese with sweet pickle.

Thea's train chugged along, through the small, pretty English towns and villages. Finally, when her sandwiches were gone and she was feeling quite bored, the train arrived into Haddenham and, as always, Aunt Fellulla was

nowhere to be seen at the station platform. Thea picked up her bags, and slowly walked to Cabbage Cottage. When she arrived, she got her key out of her bag, and opened the large, creaking door.

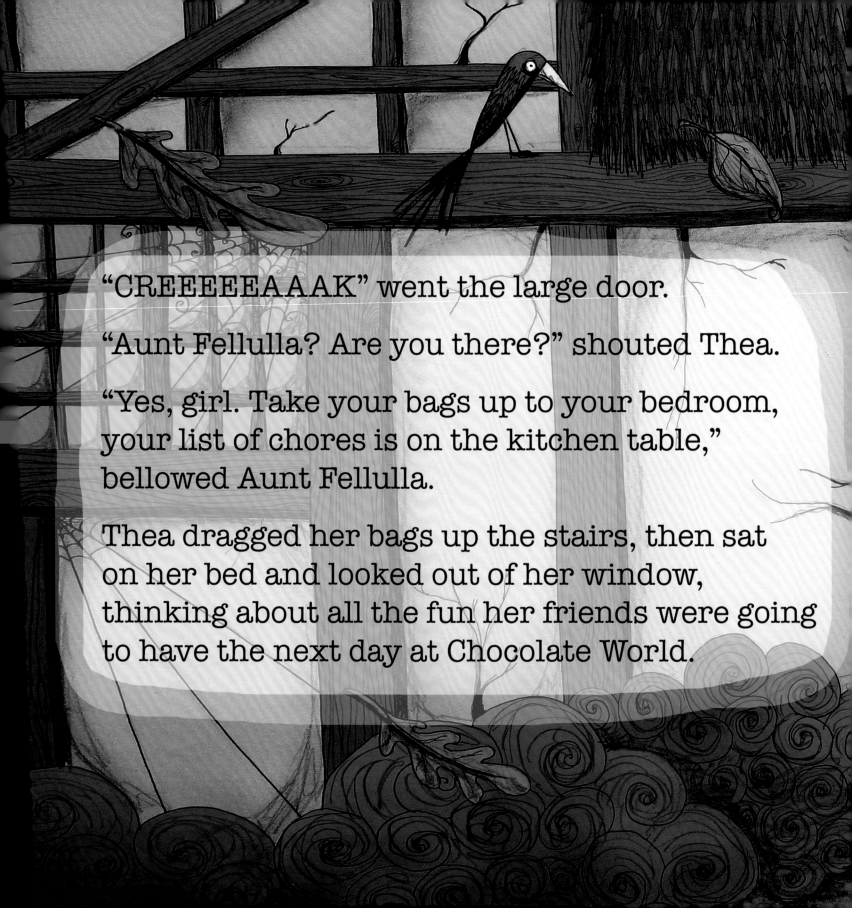

"CREEEEEAAAK" went the large door.

"Aunt Fellulla? Are you there?" shouted Thea.

"Yes, girl. Take your bags up to your bedroom, your list of chores is on the kitchen table," bellowed Aunt Fellulla.

Thea dragged her bags up the stairs, then sat on her bed and looked out of her window, thinking about all the fun her friends were going to have the next day at Chocolate World.

1. Feed Sprogget
2. Dust all of my old pictures
3. Wash up all the dirty dishes
4. Hoover the whole house
5. Clean the bathroom
6. Clean the fireplace and the chimney
7. Mow the garden
8. Bake me a pie for my dinner on Sunday
9. Go to the shops and buy my groceries for the next week
10. Wash my dirty clothes

OCTOBER

Thea went down to the kitchen to see what chores her aunt had left for her. She read the very long list, her eyes growing wide. How am I supposed to finish all of this by Sunday? she

thought to herself. Later, after saying goodbye to Aunt Fellulla, Thea went upstairs to her bedroom to get ready for bed.

When she awoke in the morning, she was thinking about her friends and what fun they were going to have.

"I so wish I could be at Chocolate World today," Thea said out loud to herself.

All of a sudden, there was a bright flash of light that seemed to come from her wardrobe. A little afraid, but mostly curious, Thea walked over to it, and opened the door very slowly. There was another bright flash of light, which made her jump backwards and land in a heap on the floor.

Thea looked up and saw the most beautiful lady she had ever seen.

"Hello, I'm Savannah, your super sweet fairy godmother!" said the lady.

She waved her glittering wand in the air, sprinkling sparkles everywhere!

"I'm here to make your sweet dreams come true, my dear Thea."

Thea stood up and realised that her fairy godmother had transformed her into a super cool new outfit.

"WOW, thank you, Fairy Godmother."

"You're welcome, my dear, it's time to go now."

"Go? Go where?" Thea asked. "I can't go anywhere until all of my chores are finished."

They went downstairs to the kitchen, and the fairy godmother waved her wand over the list of chores.

"Make this house spick and span,
clean those tables, pots and pans.
Sweep the floor with the brush,
make it clean, we're in a rush."

Thea watched in amazement as the fairy godmother's magic fed and brushed the cat and hoovered the carpets. The duster wiped all the surfaces and cleaned the pictures, while the mop frantically began cleaning the kitchen floor.

"Now it's time for us to leave."

Her super sweet fairy godmother waved her magic wand once again.

"The house is clean, your wish was heard, it's now time for Chocolate World!"

All of a sudden, Thea and her fairy godmother were whizzing through the sky. Thea looked down and could see a very large building below them. She could see a funfair wheel and a long winding river with chocolate flowing instead of water. Thea and her fairy godmother landed outside a large brown door.

The letters on the door spelled 'Chocolate World'.
The door slowly opened.

"CREEEEEAAAAK"

A tall man with bushy blonde hair, dressed in a gold suit with purple shoes greeted them.

"Hello ladies, I've been waiting for you," said the very tall man.

"My name is Lord Sweetington, welcome to my chocolate World."

Thea and her super sweet fairy godmother followed Lord Sweetington through the door and into the magical world hidden inside.

At the end of the hall, Lord Sweetington pointed to a small door.

"The magic begins when you go through this door," he said.

"But the door is tiny!" said Thea. "I'll never fit through there!"

"Not everything in this building is as it seems," replied Lord Sweetington with a large smile.

Thea opened the door and somehow fit through it easily. She stepped into a magical world with a long chocolate river and lots of beautiful sweet-covered houses.

Giggling with delight, Thea skipped down the hill, then she ate flowers, drank from candy mushrooms and rode on a merry go round made entirely from chocolate!

Hours later, when Thea was feeling really quite full and tired, she found Mr Sweetington.

"Thank you very much Sir, it's been a wonderful day," said Thea.

"We must be on our way back to Cabbage Cottage," said her super sweet fairy godmother, holding a bag of chocolate to take with them.

The fairy godmother waved her magic wand and said:

"With a swish of my wand,
And away we go.
We must return,
To the place we call home."

Thea and her fairy godmother whizzed through the night sky, back to her bedroom at Cabbage Cottage.

With a wink to Thea, the super sweet fairy godmother stepped into the wardrobe and with a flash of light she was gone!

Thea fed Sprogget the cat, then got into bed, feeling like the happiest girl in the world.

Goodnight!